Zara's Hats

* Paul Meisel *

PUFFIN BOOKS

To Grandma Zara,
the world's best grandma

PUFFIN BOOKS
Published by the Penguin Group
Penguin Young Readers Group, 345 Hudson Street, New York, New York 10014, U.S.A.
Penguin Group (Canada), 10 Alcorn Avenue, Toronto, Ontario, Canada M4V 3B2 (a division of Pearson Penguin Canada Inc.)
Penguin Books Ltd, 80 Strand, London WC2R 0RL, England
Penguin Ireland, 25 St Stephen's Green, Dublin 2, Ireland (a division of Penguin Books Ltd)
Penguin Group (Australia), 250 Camberwell Road, Camberwell, Victoria 3124, Australia (a division of Pearson Australia Group Pty Ltd)
Penguin Books India Pvt Ltd, 11 Community Centre, Panchsheel Park, New Delhi - 110 017, India
Penguin Group (NZ), Cnr Airborne and Rosedale Roads, Albany, Auckland,
New Zealand (a division of Pearson New Zealand Ltd)
Penguin Books (South Africa) (Pty) Ltd, 24 Sturdee Avenue, Rosebank, Johannesburg 2196, South Africa

Registered Offices: Penguin Books Ltd, 80 Strand, London WC2R 0RL, England

First published in the United States of America by Dutton Children's Books, a division of Penguin Putnam Books for Young Readers, 2003
Published by Puffin Books, a division of Penguin Young Readers Group, 2005

1 3 5 7 9 10 8 6 4 2

Copyright © Paul Meisel, 2003
All rights reserved

CIP Data is available.

Puffin Books ISBN 0-14-240274-5
Manufactured in China

Selig, the hatmaker, loved to make hats. Zara, his daughter, loved to help him.

Every day after school, Zara would rush home to the tiny apartment above the hat shop and drop off her books. Then she would hurry downstairs to join her mother, Leonora, and her father in the workroom, where the sewing machine always whirred and the heavy iron hissed.

Zara loved the feel of the soft fabrics as she cut them. She loved the texture of the shiny ribbons when she tied large, loopy bows. And oh, the feathers! Selig's hats were famous for having the most exquisite feathers.

"Glue this feather like so," Selig would tell her. "Then put these two over here like this, and now it's done."

"Another masterpiece, Papa!" Zara always said, trying on the finished hat.

"Good enough for the president's wife!" her father would agree. "Bravo, my clever Zara!"

"Isn't life wonderful?" Selig often asked.

And life was wonderful. The bell on the hat-shop door jingled busily.

"Oh, Mr. Selig, you are a genius!" Loretta Falsetta, the famous opera singer, trilled whenever she bought a hat.

"This hat will be perfect for the firefighters' ball!" exclaimed
Brenda Hookenlader, the fire chief's wife.

"What an extraordinary hat this is!" declared Frances Fuzzbottom,
the famous dog breeder. "Look, puppies, do you like it?"

One day, Zara was decorating a hat for the fire chief's wife. "Two more red feathers and it will be another masterpiece," she said to her father.

"I'm afraid there are no more red," he replied. "But use these two yellow ones. I'm sure you'll do something clever with them—good enough for Mrs. Hookenlader, or even the president's wife. Tomorrow I will buy more."

A few days later, Zara raced home only to find the lights out in the shop and her father sitting at his cutting table, looking sad.

"What's the matter, Papa?" she asked.

"It's the feathers, Zara dear," answered Selig. "I'm afraid we've run out."

"But can't you get more?"

"I've tried everywhere," Selig said with a sigh. "There seem to be no more feathers anywhere in the city."

It wasn't long before there were no more hats in Selig's shop, either.

SELIG'S HATS

SORRY
NO HATS

As each day passed, he grew more melancholy. He needed to make hats to be happy, and he needed feathers to make hats.

Finally, Selig couldn't stand it anymore. If the feathers wouldn't come to him, he would have to go to the feathers.

"Don't worry, my darlings," he said to Zara and Leonora as he boarded a steamer headed for far-off places. "I will return with many fine feathers, and the bell on the hat-shop door will once again be jingling."

Selig sailed for many weeks. The rough seas made him seasick.

He traveled by elephant...

and camel…

and dugout canoe…

but wherever he was, he always sent Zara and Leonora postcards, so
they would know he was thinking of them.

Meanwhile, Zara and her mother were missing Selig terribly.
Zara's heart sank each day when she returned home from school and
saw the empty shop window.

To cheer themselves up, Zara and her mother took long walks in the park.

Zara fed bits of bread to the ducks and swooped up and down on the carousel.

Sometimes she joined a group of children watching a puppet show or bought hot roasted chestnuts from the cart man.

But absolutely nothing could take the place of her father.

Then one day, on the way home from the park, Zara had an idea.

She ran through the empty hat shop directly to the little work-room, where she began cutting leaves out of fabric and gluing them to wire. She twisted brightly colored ribbons into flowers of all sorts.

She modeled her favorite fruits and animals out of papier-mâché. When they were dry, Zara painted them with the brightest colors in her paint box. Next she sewed and pinned and glued what she had made to some of her father's unfinished hats.

She arranged the hats on the empty stands in the shop window.
"There," she said. "Now it's not so lonely."

When Zara came home from school the next day, a small crowd
was gathered in front of the little hat shop.

"I simply must have that hat in the window," said Mrs. Zernockel as Zara let her inside. "It will make my nose look less pink."

"And that one is precious!" exclaimed Dolly McFizzle. "I don't know where it came from, but it is divine. Please wrap it up!"

"My cats will simply adore this hat," purred Miss Katrina Katnip.

"You want to buy these hats?" asked Zara.

"Yes!" shouted the women.

In no time at all, Zara had the hats in boxes, and the window was empty once again.

That night, Zara and her mother made new hats, and the next day, those hats, too, were sold.

Word spread quickly. Everyone loved Zara's hats.

Not long after that, Selig returned from his journey, his heart swelling with joy at the thought of seeing his family again. Nevertheless, he was worried, too. He had not been able to find a single feather to bring back. What would they do?

But as he approached the little hat shop, he was shocked by what he saw. It was not empty and dark, as he had expected. Instead, the window was filled with the most amazing hats he had ever seen, and the shop was crowded with customers.

"Papa!" shouted Zara when the little bell jingled and she saw her father coming through the door.

"Oh, how I missed you," Selig said, wrapping his arms around Zara in a big hug. "And my dear wife, too." He smiled at Leonora and kissed her warmly. "But what has happened here?" He looked around in astonishment. "What hats are these?"

"The empty hat stands made me sad, Papa," said Zara. "So I decorated some hats and put them in the window."

The hat shop suddenly became very quiet. "I thought these were from Paris," said Mrs. Fezzleworth. "*You* made these extraordinary hats?"

"Why, yes," replied Zara. "I hope you're not mad at me, Papa."

Selig looked around at the fabulous hats and at all of the happy customers.

"Mad? How could I be mad? These hats are amazing. Stupendous. I am so proud of you," he exclaimed. "Even the president's wife would love them. Bravo, my clever Zara!"

Everyone in the hat shop clapped, except for Loretta Falsetta, who trilled.

From that day on, Selig, Leonora, and Zara kept the hat shop filled with Zara's hats. Who needed feathers? People came from near and far to see the little hatmaker and to buy her hats—

bakers and duchesses, mountain climbers and firefighters, musicians, veterinarians, baseball players, and...

...even the president's wife.